THE CRUISERS

THE CRU

SERS

WALTER DEAN MYERS

SCHOLASTIC PRESS ▪ NEW YORK

TO M. JERRY WEISS
—W. D. M.

All rights reserved. Published by Scholastic Press, an imprint of Scholastic Inc., *Publishers since 1920.* SCHOLASTIC, SCHOLASTIC PRESS, and associated logos are trademarks and/or registered trademarks of Scholastic Inc.

No part of this publication may be reproduced, stored in a retrieval system, or transmitted in any form or by any means, electronic, mechanical, photocopying, recording, or otherwise, without written permission of the publisher. For information regarding permission, write to Scholastic Inc., Attention: Permissions Department, 557 Broadway, New York, NY 10012.

CIP available

ISBN 978-0-439-91626-4

10 9 8 7 6 5 4 3 2 1   10 11 12 13 14
Printed in the United States of America   23
First edition, August 2010

The display type was set in Goshen and Nova.
The text type was set in Adobe Caslon Pro.
Book design by Kristina Iulo

CHAPTER ONE
Life on the High C's

Education is a journey on the high seas of life.
— *Adrian Culpepper, Assistant Principal*

Okay, this time it was LaShonda Powell who got us into trouble. She had written an article for our group's newspaper, *The Cruiser,* she called "Life on the High C's or, Do We Really Need A's and B's?" I told her when she turned it in that Culpepper was going to blow up, but you know LaShonda. The girl just doesn't care.

The last time that Mr. Culpepper had called us to his office he said that it was going to be the very, *very* last chance we were going to have to shape up.

"He can't suspend all four of us," LaShonda said. "I mean, really, how would that look on the school's record?"

"I knew something bad was going to happen as soon as I saw that Da Vinci Academy came in fourth in the Academic Olympics," Kambui said. "We were supposed to be *numero uno!*"

"At least," Bobbi added.

I wasn't worried about Da Vinci being fourth, or even about being suspended. I was worried about being dropped from the school altogether. My grades were way down and I knew it. Da Vinci was supposed to be one of the best gifted and talented schools in the city, and I simply wasn't doing that well. It wasn't that the material we were learning was too hard. In fact, it may have been too easy, and I really didn't have to study so I was only paying attention to the stuff that interested me, which was mostly Phys Ed and Language Arts. Somehow I just couldn't wrap my head around the other classes.

When Mr. Culpepper, the assistant principal and chief executioner, came in, he did it with a flourish, breathing through his nose and looking like a cross between a really mad Santa Claus and a swishy dragon.

"Well, what are we to say this morning?" he asked, looking over his rimless glasses. "Or have the grades said enough? Hmmm?"

No response.

"We have noted two trends among this small group of miscreants," Mr. Culpepper went on. "The first is that none of you are living up to your potential. And yes, we do know your individual abilities because you have all tested very well on the IQ tests. What I strongly suspect is that you just don't care enough about education or about Da Vinci Academy for the Gifted and Talented. I'm wondering if you are really Da Vinci material."

"We care," I said. It sounded lame coming out.

"If it were left to me," Mr. Culpepper continued, raising his volume slightly, "I would stick with the idea that education is about accomplishment and not potential and suggest that you all find other schools, perhaps ones closer to your homes. But since it is the principal, Mrs. Maxwell, who is the dispenser of last chances and not I, we will continue our little adventure a bit further. And, to tell the truth, I rather like her idea. She sees it as a final opportunity to prove you belong here. I see it as enough rope. If you get my drift."

"What do we have to do?" LaShonda asked. LaShonda was tall, dark, and slightly wild-looking. Fashion design was her thing. She could make an entire outfit for anyone overnight. When we had first met in the sixth grade, she had told me that her parents had abandoned her and her younger brother when they were kids and that she lived with him in a group home in the Bronx.

"As you know, for our study of the Civil War, the entire eighth grade is being divided into Union sympathizers and Confederate sympathizers. Mrs. Maxwell, she of the compassionate heart, is appointing the four of you — what do you call yourselves? oh, yes, the Cruisers — to attempt to negotiate a peace between the two sides before war actually breaks out. It will take, in my opinion, more skill and dedication than any of you possess. But for some strange reason, she believes that by actually giving you more responsibility she will inspire you to greater efforts. I, of course, disagree."

"How are we going to stop a *war*?" Kambui asked.

"Well, perhaps Mr. Scott could take his six-foot frame, his weird hairstyle with dreads on top and Indian braids on the side, and simply make them all go home," Mr. Culpepper said. "I personally would attempt to negotiate a compromise. Maybe something can be learned from the history of the war itself, I suppose. You'll also have to have more luck than any of you deserve. But it's up to you, isn't it?"

When we left Mr. Culpepper's office we were all down. We knew what he was saying. The "one more chance" had boiled down to just that: one more chance.

"Anybody getting a bad feeling about this?" Bobbi asked in the hallway. "Sort of like he's handing out menus for a final meal?"

"Look, we've got our newspaper started," I said. "Maybe we can write a series of articles talking about how stupid war is. Let's everybody think about it overnight and have a meeting tomorrow morning before the first class."

"Maybe LaShonda shouldn't have quoted Mr. Culpepper," Kambui said.

"What we are doing, Kambui Owens, is publishing a newspaper that speaks for the real people of this school," LaShonda said. "I'm not holding back just because he's got a little power."

The Palette was the official school newspaper and Mr. Culpepper was its adviser. Ashley Schmidt was its editor and she was cool, but Mr. Culpepper had final approval on anything, and as far as I was concerned the paper was just a way of putting out school propaganda. When the school got a printer that prints eleven-by-seventeen-inch pages I came up with the idea of an alternative paper. On the masthead of *The Palette* was the quote from Mr. C.: *Education is a journey on the high seas of life.* We played off of that and said we weren't on a journey, we were just cruising. I called our newspaper *The Cruiser.* It was LaShonda's idea to call our staff — LaShonda, Bobbi, Kambui, and me — the Cruisers.

We published the paper once every two weeks unless something special happened and we put out a special edition. We tried to charge a quarter a copy but Mrs. Maxwell said we couldn't make it a commercial venture.

"And in the future" — Mr. Culpepper stepped from his office into the hall — "you will not quote me or any other teacher, official, or staff member of this school without written permission. Do you hear me?"

"Yes, O mighty one!" Bobbi said.

Mr. Culpepper started down the hall muttering something about Cruisers rhyming with *losers.*

No way we were losers, and if Mr. C. didn't know it, we did. The thing was that Da Vinci Academy was supposed to be all world. We had been written up in the *New York Times* and *Newsweek* as a Harlem school that was taking care of business. Three quarters of the kids at Da Vinci were from outside of Harlem and were into that heavy competition thing. Who got the most A's and turned in the longest papers, that kind of thing. But there were some kids who just were into the sweating and fretting jam. LaShonda called them the "real people."

LaShonda Powell lived in a home with about fifteen other kids. Every morning she had to take her little brother to school in the West Bronx and then had to take the train downtown to Harlem to go to Da Vinci. She was late three or four times a week.

Barbara McCall was a math whiz and played second board on the chess team. She scored straight A's in Algebra but D's in about everything else. Everybody called her Bobbi.

Kambui Owens, my main man, lived with his grandmother a few blocks from me. Sometimes, when his father was out of jail, he lived with them. Kambui was deep into photography and I figured he had the best chance of becoming famous one day.

My name is Alexander Scott, but my friends call me Zander. Language Arts is my thing and one day I'd like to write screenplays. I don't really have serious issues but I can't seem to get myself to deal with the work. I usually liked Da Vinci because there weren't a lot of fights. I couldn't stand the kids who were snobby just because they had the smart thing going on. I don't like snobby people.

I was hoping things were going to work out, even if Mr. Culpepper was ready to come down on us real hard. Mrs. Maxwell, the principal, was good people and she gave us as many breaks as she could. But if I did have to leave Da Vinci I didn't think it would be the end of the world. At least I didn't until I got home that evening.

THE CRUISER

LIFE ON THE HIGH C's

Education is a journey on the high seas of life.

— Adrian Culpepper, Assistant Principal

By LaShonda Powell

We are all glad that we are taking a journey on the high seas of life with Adrian and his crew. But why do we have to mess up every day by struggling to get an A or a B when a good, strong C will do? When we are out in the world will anybody know what grades we got in the eighth grade? Will anybody care? Although "balance" begins with *B* and *A*, the *C* near the end of the word is just as important. And from LaShonda's point of view both the *B* and the *A* are working too hard to get noticed. *A* shows up twice and *B* has pushed its way to the front. *The Cruiser* thinks that life should be laid-back and enjoyed.

CHAPTER TWO
Gone with the Breeze

My moms was at the table checking herself out in the hand mirror she always had around. She had this weird thing on her head that might have been a hat and her eyes looked a little red, like she had been crying or something.

"So what do you have on your head?" I asked her.

"Mickey Mouse ears," she said. "You like them?"

"Yo, I'm falling out," I said. "What do you have them on for?"

"They were lying on a set today," Mom said. "Would you be embarrassed if I had to wear Mickey Mouse ears in a film?"

"Not really," I said, searching in the back of the refrigerator for jelly. "You got a new job?"

"Not quite," she said.

If you read any of the black magazines you have probably seen my moms. She's pretty and she does modeling. Usually she's just smiling and holding up a tube of toothpaste or a bar of soap. Sometimes she's only wearing her underwear and I don't like that because I don't like guys in the school saying that my mom is hot.

If you live in Seattle or Portland you might have seen my father on television. His name is Donald Scott and he's a weatherman. My parents were divorced when I was four and I don't remember my father living with us. He got married again and has another kid, a girl. He sends me gift certificates to bookstores on my birthday and at Christmas and if he's in New York he'll call the house to see if I want to see him. Usually I don't. Everybody thinks that he has two voices, one for television and one that he uses the rest of the time. He doesn't. Whenever he talks it sounds like he's announcing his life and any moment he's going to break out with the weather forecast. It's not that I don't get along with the dude. I do, but I like my mom better even if I'm not supposed to choose one over the other.

"Work is work. Isn't that what you always say?" I asked Mom.

"This is different." She had on a long face, which meant something was bothering her.

"And?"

"And Marc thinks he can get me a part in a new comedy film," she said. "They're going to shoot it outside of Savannah, Georgia, so I'd have to go down there. You okay with that?"

"Sure."

"What would you be doing if I went away for two months for a shoot?" she asked.

"Drinking beer and having pizza parties," I said. "What else?"

"I'm serious," Mom said.

"If you got a part in a movie how come you're not excited?" I asked. "They want you to take your clothes off?"

"Would I be in a movie where I took my clothes off?" she asked. "Would I?"

"Then why are you acting like something's wrong?"

"This is supposed to be a remake of *Gone with the Wind*," Mom said. "But it's supposed to be satire. You know, funny."

"So?"

"And I'm supposed to be Scarlett O'Hara's maid," she said. "How would you feel about that?"

"I don't care," I said. "How do you feel about it?"

"Marc thinks I can do comedy."

"Then do it," I said.

Marc was Mom's agent. He wasn't that good an agent as far as I was concerned but he was good at basketball. He had a tryout for the Nets once but hurt his ankle the week before and didn't get a chance for it to heal before the tryout. I was used to Mom trying to get jobs, mostly in commercials, so it didn't matter to me.

"You wouldn't really drink beer, right?" she asked. "At least not until you're sixteen?"

"I guess," I said.

"Did I tell you that I got a subpoena today?"

"A what?"

"Your father has decided that he wants to have custody of you," Mom said. "He thinks I can't . . ."

She started tearing up.

"Can he do that?" I asked.

"You know she's a teacher, right?"

The "she" was my father's wife. "I just won't go," I said.

"He keeps asking me how you're doing and I keep saying fine, but then he called the school."

"That was sneaky," I said.

"He's always been a little sneaky. So now I have to send him a sworn statement about your progress, your health, and your education," Mom said. "I don't think he can force me to give you up, but . . ."

She looked a little panicky. Like the time the rent was way overdue and the landlord started banging on the door. He was just being a pain in the butt and I think he wanted to hit on her. She's pretty tough when she's right, but sometimes things get her down and she starts talking about how she should take a job as a waitress or a nurse's aide.

What my mom has going on is that she's flat-out beautiful. Okay, so she's hot. But jobs are hard to get and when she doesn't get work for a while she starts to lose confidence. I can understand that.

"I think everything is going to be all right," I said. "You want me to call his wife and tell her that I hate her?"

"Oh, Alexander, you'll love Seattle," Mom said, holding

her nose and talking like my father's wife. "The air is so much fresher out here than it is in New York and the view across the sound is too, too wonderful."

I love it when Mom does imitations. She's good at them and it takes her out of her bad moods. Not enough to stop her from burning the mac and cheese she made for supper, but enough so that she wasn't crying.

The next morning I got up early and took my bike to school. We have racks outside in the back that you are allowed to use if you show up wearing a helmet.

When I got in the building I saw LaShonda talking to Shantese Hopkins in the hallway. Shantese thinks she's got it going on. She does but I pretend not to notice it. So I just nodded at her when I pushed past some noisy sixth-graders to get to where they were standing.

"Did you hear what Ashley had the nerve to publish in *The Palette*?" LaShonda asked. "And right across from the sports page so everybody was sure to see it?"

"What?"

"A guest editorial by Alvin McCraney and the 'Sons of the Confederacy' saying that he thinks the Southern states should break away from the Union so they can continue their job of civilizing the Negroes. I'm definitely ready to go to war with that dude."

"He actually wrote that?"

"Yeah!" LaShonda said.

Okay, so Da Vinci has a black principal, and two black teachers, but only about thirty black students out of almost three hundred. Ten in the eighth grade, a few in the seventh, and a bunch of sixth-graders. Everybody got along well, with most of the kids being into whatever their talents were about.

"It's probably just about this Civil War project," I answered.

"All I know is that I didn't like it," LaShonda said.

The Palette was a good paper that sometimes ran guest editorials or cartoons. Ashley was smart and hip. Usually she published stories about the school's activities, such as sports, drama programs, and upcoming events. But once in a while she would run something that would shake things up. Once she ran an interview with a guy on trial for selling drugs who said that crack should be legalized, and once she did a piece saying that schools should be open at night for homeless people to sleep in.

"If we're supposed to be peacemakers I guess we're neutral," I said.

"Can we just kill Alvin and then start being neutral from there?" LaShonda asked.

I could see that peacemaking wasn't going to be as easy as it seemed.

THE PALETTE
Guest Editorial

We believe that it is our sacred duty to our brothers of African descent to continue teaching them our ways, including our religion, our principles, and our civilization. Why, go to a Northern city, such as New York, and you will see the black inhabitants of that city lying around in a most unseemly way. Often they will inhabit the worst quarters of the city and behave in a way that would not be tolerated below the Mason-Dixon Line.

In many cities whose newspapers rally behind the abolitionist banner we find Negroes being loud and boisterous on the streets, going into and out of places where alcohol is sold, and acting in as heathen a manner as they did on their native African shores.

We believe that we must protect the Negro race from those who, in the name of freedom, would turn them loose in an uncaring society and expect them to compete against white men.

We believe we owe it to these visitors to our shore to continue bringing them along, civilizing them as we give them opportunities for honest labor and the fruits of our fair country. To this end and this end alone, we owe it to ourselves to break the treaty with the Northern states and to do our duty as Southerners.

— *Alvin McCraney and the Sons of the Confederacy*

CHAPTER THREE

Free Speech on the Menu,
with a Side Order of Knuckle Stew

We were supposed to be planning our negotiations between the Union and the Confederacy but ended up talking about what Alvin had written.

"We have to make a move on that dude. He's talking about freedom of speech and stuff but what he's really dealing with is race," Kambui said as we sat in the lunchroom. "He's putting out his little piece in *The Palette* and then cracking up on it. I think he needs a serious beat down."

"Who we beating up?" Cody Weinstein came to the table and threw a leg over the back of a chair.

"Alvin," Kambui said. "You see what he wrote in the school paper?"

"Yeah, I saw it. Why don't you just go to Mrs. Maxwell

and say you object to the piece," Cody said. "She's got to go for it."

"Culpepper is on Alvin's side," Kambui said. He had his toothpick working big-time. "I told him about the article and he said it was about freedom of speech. I don't think we should let him get away with it. What you thinking, Zander?"

"Let's have a meeting with Alvin," I said. "If this is supposed to be about the Civil War, then we need to deal with the issues. Race was part of that whole thing."

"That's what Alvin's saying, man." Kambui was getting mad. "But you should have seen how the guys on the soccer team were reading the piece in the lunchroom and cracking up."

"How did people deal with that stuff before the Civil War?" LaShonda asked.

"The South said they had a constitutional right to have slaves," Bobbi said. "And they did."

"You can't have a constitutional right to own somebody!" LaShonda said.

"The Confederate states thought they had it and that it was guaranteed by the Constitution," Cody said. "That's why they went to war. Did you ever read their Declarations of Causes of Secession that Mr. Siegfried assigned?"

No, I hadn't. I didn't really know anything about the Civil War except for what I had seen in the movies or on television. What I was thinking was that I didn't want to deal with Alvin. I wanted to deal with the Civil War, do a good job on that, and move on. As far as I was concerned, Mr. Culpepper had to be on our side.

To see Mr. Culpepper you had to write him a note asking him to meet with you and telling him what you wanted to talk about. In the note, I wrote that I needed to set up an official meeting between the Cruisers and Alvin McCraney as soon as possible.

I didn't really know Alvin. He played goalie on the soccer team and was supposed to be hard. He had been in one of my Language Arts classes in the seventh grade and he was pretty smart. But all the students at Da Vinci had the smart thing going on, so it wasn't a big deal.

School seemed to drag all afternoon and a lot of the kids were rapping about what Alvin had written. Ashley had things stirred up again.

I knew I had to write something for *The Cruiser*. I had Media Studies so I could hang out in the library, and I tried working on a piece. At first everything I was writing sounded too mad, but when I started making it look less mad it was sounding lame.

"Hey, Zander, what's happening?" Sidney Aronofsky asked.

"Nothing much," I said, putting my piece aside. "How you doing?"

"Okay, okay," Sidney said. "Look, I just want you to know that I didn't like that piece in *The Palette*. I don't think whoever wrote it was right, and I don't think that I should have to be held up as a racist because I'm white or because my folks are from the South."

"Who said that you were a racist?"

"Nobody said it," Sidney said. "But when something like that comes out it makes you either try to ignore it or you slide to one side or the other. You know what I mean?"

"Yes, sort of," I said.

Sidney was at Da Vinci because of his general grades and the fact that he had played chess in the nationals. He was Mr. Culpepper's ideal student. His grades were good and at least once a year he was featured in some newspaper because of his chess. He was also one of the four best under-sixteen players in New York.

Okay, the picture was getting clearer. I hadn't thought much about it when LaShonda first mentioned it but I did see some of the other white soccer players clowning around in the hallway and I figured they were getting off on what Alvin had written. They were laughing and joking around in the hallway and whenever a black or Latino kid came by they would put their heads down like they were hiding something. The white kids, like Sidney, were taking it seriously, too.

At two-thirty, the last announcements of the day came over the loudspeaker. Usually, the announcements were just about what team was practicing, or sometimes a teacher would remind us what paper was due the next day. The announcement that came over the loudspeaker after I had given Mr. Culpepper the note surprised me. A girl announced that the Cruisers and the Sons of the Confederacy were to meet in Mr. Culpepper's office at eight-thirty in the morning.

Bobbi met me in the hallway near the front door.

"Who are the Sons of the Confederacy?" she asked.

"It's got to be something Alvin dreamed up," I said. "But I guess if we can be the Cruisers they can be the Sons of the Confederacy."

"You getting nervous?" she asked.

"No," I lied.

"I am, too," she said, smiling her squinchy-eyed smile. "But it's good we're getting our first meeting so soon, right?"

"Right."

THE CRUISER

OP-ED TO THE SONS OF THE CONFEDERACY

By Zander Scott

What are we talking about when we use words like "civilized"? Are we talking about just getting people to do what we want them to do and act the way we want, or are we allowing them the full range of experiences that we would allow ourselves? If someone takes a man from his home and family and forces him to work in the cotton fields of Georgia against his will, who is the more civilized? Is it the man who has stolen a human being or the man working in the field who cannot read or write English because the person who stole him has made it impossible for him to do so?

Is forcing another person into slavery civilized? Perhaps the black people working in the fields should rise up and do the same as has been done to them — break up families, steal the people, and whip and kill those who protest. Would this show that they have become "civilized" because they have copied their masters?

The Cruiser doesn't think so!

CHAPTER FOUR
Zander and the Bear

Kambui had seen a lens he wanted for his camera in a junk shop and I walked him there. All the way he was talking about Alvin, and I could see that it was bothering him a lot.

"In a way, when somebody says they don't like you," he said, "you don't really have a good comeback."

"Then we have to come up with one," I said.

We reached the shop and the guy still wanted more for the lens than Kambui wanted to pay. I got the feeling that the guy was making fun of Kambui because he was so young. Adults dance down that street sometimes.

Kambui was mad at the guy in the shop, at Alvin, and I think he was getting mad with me by the time we split up.

When I got home there was a note on the refrigerator

that I should make my own supper and that there were leftovers in the fridge if I wanted them. I found five small bowls of leftover veggies, some Chinese food in a paper carton, a piece of fried chicken wrapped in aluminum foil, and two little round cups of some kind of sauce. Not bad. I put the Chinese food and the fried chicken on a plate and zapped it in the microwave.

I had to read the beginning of *A Raisin in the Sun* by Lorraine Hansberry for Language Arts the next day so I got out my iPod, put on the television, and was just starting it when the phone rang. It was Kambui.

"So you know you got to be strong tomorrow when we face Alvin and his crew," he said.

"What's that mean?" I asked.

"It means he got some of the other guys on the soccer team to join up with him," Kambui said. "That's what that Sons of the Confederacy thing is about. He's showing he got some muscle with his hustle."

"No problem," I said. "Just because you're strong don't mean you're not wrong. And Alvin is about as wrong as he can get."

"Okay, but remember what my grandfather used to say," Kambui said. "You meet a bear in the woods and he's not supposed to be there, it still won't make any difference on the menu. You're going to be lunch."

I was beginning to feel a little like somebody's lunch.

The thing was that I had never thought a lot about being African American. I mean, there I was, black from locks to 'Boks, from dreads to Keds, but I just didn't think much on it and now it was all up in my face. I definitely needed to get my head together.

Ten. Ten soccer players, and all wearing gray hats, the kind you buy in novelty shops that have a little Confederate flag on the side. They were sitting under the American flag in Mr. Culpepper's office when the Cruisers and I came in. Alvin looked me up and down like I was short or something and I thought about what Kambui had said about the bear. I felt a little nervous, but I knew I was correct.

"So what did you gentlemen want to see us about?" Alvin spoke with this drawl that kind of cracked me up.

"About what you wrote in *The Palette*," I said. "I think that was wrong and I think you knew it was wrong."

"Well, we're edging toward secession," Alvin went on. "You people have your ideas and we have ours. You're entitled to spread yours as you see fit. We intend to do the same."

"Talking about civilizing Negroes?" Bobbi spoke up. "That's your idea?"

"You think they can't be civilized?" Billy Stroud asked.

Billy Stroud was short, as wide as he was tall, and a bully who was always fighting some kid either smaller than him or who just wasn't into the physical thing. I looked at him and he was grinning like all the other ballplayers.

"I see you don't have any black ballplayers in your Sons of the Shredded Wheatacy or whatever you call yourselves," LaShonda said.

"You can't pronounce your words well enough to say 'Confederacy'?" Alvin asked.

"Maybe what you need is a beat down," Kambui said. "Maybe if you got a beat down you could understand LaShonda better."

"Whoa!" Mr. Culpepper stood and raised both hands in the air. "This is supposed to be a meeting of two groups interested in preventing war. Not two groups threatening each other. Mr. Scott, I thought you people were supposed to be peacekeepers."

"We're trying to be peaceful," I said. "That's why we called the meeting."

"But if you don't want peace," Billy spoke up again, "we can go anyway you want to take it."

"Yo, Billy, shut up!" Kambui said.

"Yo, Kambui, shut me up!" Billy came back.

"The meeting is over!" Mr. Culpepper was speaking as loud as I had ever heard him. "Cruisers, leave first."

I was mad when I left. Not so much mad at Alvin and his Sons of the Confederacy, but mad at myself for not having a better program to deal with him. A problem had come up and I was supposed to be representing and I had just stood there feeling stupid.

"They were just talking big because Zander came off so weak," Kambui said.

"You did come off weak," LaShonda said. "They're putting race all in the game and Cody is saying we should get ready to throw down instead of you. I think you're scared."

"No, I'm not scared," I said. "But what are you going to win if you fight them? If I'm going to have a fight I got to see the win in it so I'll know what I'm fighting for."

"How about some r-e-s-p-e-c-t, pretty boy?" LaShonda was mad as she walked away from me. "It's in the dictionary!"

We met up with Cody in the hall.

Kambui followed LaShonda and Cody headed for the gym for his next class, leaving me and Bobbi standing in the middle of the hallway.

"I'll probably get killed, but I got your back if we have to fight," she said.

How America got into the Civil War in the first place was getting clearer and clearer. People were just taking sides and stumbling to the rumbling. Cody, Kambui, LaShonda, and even Bobbi were ready to start fighting and we weren't even all that clear what the issues were.

Mr. Siegfried had all the past reading assignments in a notebook on his desk and I went to his room to check it out.

"You understand that the reading assignments are actually in books," Mr. Siegfried said as I copied down some of the ones I had missed. "That's the thing made out of paper with little numbers at the bottom of each page?"

"Yes, sir." Me, feeling stupid.

In less than two minutes in Mr. Culpepper's office the Cruisers had turned from being peacekeepers to not only fighting among ourselves but planning a battle against the soccer team. To begin with, there were ten of them against four of us. The odds didn't look good.

I went to Language Arts, but I couldn't concentrate on what Miss LoBretto was saying. First I was thinking of all the things I should have said in Mr. Culpepper's office, and then I began thinking about fighting Alvin. I knew I was faster than he was, but I didn't know if I could beat him.

After Language Arts I had a study period and was hoping I didn't run into any of the other Cruisers until I had thought of a new plan.

"Alexander, are you headed toward the cafeteria?" It was Mrs. Maxwell.

"Sort of," I said.

"Mr. Culpepper said that things didn't work out too well at your meeting this morning," Mrs. Maxwell said as we walked down the hall. "He thinks it's maybe a bad idea to have groups of students within the school representing the North and the South and against each other. Even if it is a school exercise. What do you think?"

"Could be," I said.

"You know, of course, that before the Civil War the abolitionists, those people who thought slavery was morally wrong, tried to convince the slaveholders to end the practice," Mrs. Maxwell spoke softly. "But the slaveholders thought it was to their advantage to keep slavery. The abolitionists didn't give up just because it was difficult, though. I rather admire them for that. Don't you?"

"Yeah, I guess so. I mean, yes, ma'am."

"And the black people being held in bondage didn't give up," Mrs. Maxwell said. "They escaped when they could and resisted when they could. Didn't they?"

"Yes, ma'am."

"So what's going to be your next move?" our principal asked.

"I'll think of something," I said.

"I thought you would," Mrs. Maxwell said. "Having peacekeepers around is a very good idea."

"Mrs. Maxwell, if we can't find a way of stopping the Civil War, is it going to look bad for the Cruisers — I mean for me, LaShonda, Kambui, and Bobbi —"

"For those students who aren't doing as well as they might?" she asked.

"Yes, ma'am."

"Oh, I don't know. Sometimes things are difficult to resolve," Mrs. Maxwell said. "But those difficulties often supply great opportunities for people to prove themselves. Don't you think?"

"Or mess up," I said.

"Or, as you say, mess up," Mrs. Maxwell said. "But I don't think you'll mess up. I think you'll do rather well."

Mrs. Maxwell went into the cafeteria and I went on down to the media center. I was surprised when she had told me that Mr. Culpepper had wanted to stop the North and South groups. But it did look like we were headed for a showdown.

I knew if my mother was my age she would have been like LaShonda, ready to fight. My father would have gone into his television thing. He had this real formal voice that he used when he gave the weather.

The temperature is expected to reach the mid fifties tomorrow with a thirty percent chance of precipitation. If the rain holds up past eleven-thirty we will commence the Battle of Gettysburg.

You could listen to him for an hour and not remember one thing he said. His wife always wanted to speak to me over the phone, to ask me questions about how my ball playing was going or what computer games I liked to play. I didn't really hate her, but I didn't want to talk to her or him on the phone.

The thing that got to me was how Alvin and the other soccer players were speaking with accents and making the whole thing seem like some kind of joke. The joking around was something they could kind of hide behind. They were turning up the tension with smiles on their faces.

We had to find a way to change that.

THE CRUISER

THE THERAPEUTIC VALUE OF AN

OLD-FASHIONED BEAT DOWN

By Kambui Owens

In my opinion, electroshock has been given a bad name because people associate pain with medicine and think it has to be wrong. Recently, I have seen articles that suggest that electroshock did have some value. What I am wondering is if a good old-fashioned beat down might not have some value as well.

Usually, people know when they are being gob-slobbering foul. But you can't talk to them because they are so into their foulness they don't hear you. So what a beat down could accomplish is to get the people you are trying to reach to actually pay attention to you. In a lot of the pictures from the Civil War you see soldiers lying in the fields stone-dead. Okay, when you shoot a dude you certainly get his attention. He knows you are all about Serious with a capital *S*, and he will start to pay attention unless he is an S-hole. Now, I am against shooting people but I do think that maybe we can approach the same effect with a beat down. When people are facedown with a bloody lip or a tooth lying on the ground next to them they will get the idea that they need to put some giddyap in their listen up.

Maybe a whole lot of people needed to be killed during the Civil War before General Robert E. Lee came around to seeing the light. Maybe the Sons of the Confederacy have to go through some changes before they start seeing the light.

I am not suggesting violence. What I'm saying is that we look into the possibility that the laying on of hands just might have some therapeutic value.

Yeah, he did." Kambui was on the phone and it was definitely a party line because I could hear his attitude was on with him. "Ashley didn't want him running another guest editorial so now the Sons of the Confederacy are putting out their own newspaper. They've photocopied a real newspaper from 1807, *The Charleston Courier*, with ads in it about buying slaves. They Photoshopped a picture of Alvin and put that on the front page. He's pushing the whole thing real hard. He's thinking we don't have the heart to do anything about it."

"It's a real newspaper?"

"Mr. Siegfried said it was one of the biggest Southern newspapers before the Civil War," Kambui said. "So he's saying he's just putting out copies of a historical document."

"So what you want to do?" I asked.

"Throw down!" Kambui said. "If he knows we're not going to go upside his head then he's just going to keep running with it."

"And if we beat him up we'll get suspended," I said.

"Yeah, right," Kambui agreed. "I'm glad you're finally getting the point because we're in the same position the slaves were in. I think the least thing you could do would be to quit as head of the Cruisers. Maybe come on out in the cotton fields with the rest of us."

Click.

Click? I looked at the phone. Kambui had hung up on me. He was challenging me when he knew that what he was saying about beating up Alvin wasn't going to work. I could dig him getting frustrated, though, and they were looking at me to do something.

The thing was that Alvin was tiptoeing around on the edges of the affair and maybe it would eventually come to blows the way Kambui wanted. But I could see something else going on, too. Alvin might have been tiptoeing but some of the other guys on the soccer team were beginning to kick it big-time.

Later at school, on the second floor, Billy Stroud caught Demetrius Brown coming out of the media center, grabbed him by the wrist, and started acting like he was auctioning him off.

"What am I offered for this fine young boy? We're starting at one hundred dollars. Do I hear one fifty? Two hundred?"

Demetrius didn't know what was going on. Some of the kids stopped to see what was happening and some walked away really fast. I went over to Stroud and pushed him against the wall.

"What are you doing, man?" I asked him. We were nose to nose.

I could feel my heart beating faster when Billy leaned in to me so that our chests were touching.

"What you push me for?" he asked.

"You know why," I said. "What more you need me to do?"

He looked around, saw all the kids looking at him, and then waved me off. "Punk!"

I wanted to go after him, to punch him in the face, to do something. I was getting to feel like Kambui now, but I knew all the things I had said to him were true. If

I was going to fight Billy Stroud, or anybody, I had to see a win in it somewhere, not just the satisfaction of a few swings.

My first idea was that I needed to calm Kambui down so he wouldn't get kicked out of school, and then deal with Alvin and Billy and anyone else who was starting trouble. Then I thought that I really needed Alvin to chill so that Kambui would calm down, and that would get me some time to think about what the Cruisers could do.

We had basketball practice, and some of the soccer players came to the gym. I knew what they were doing. Billy had got them to come with him for backup. I knew that what every bully needed was to make sure that if there was a fight it would go down on his terms. I wasn't going to let that happen.

I was okay in basketball, and I thought I had a chance against Billy, but I needed to think things through first. In a way I knew that Billy was winning the set because all I could think of was throwing hands. That had to be a loss.

We had a good practice, and when we went to the locker room Billy followed me in.

"I heard you were tough," he said. "I just came to see what kind of body you have."

"It's black, and it ain't slack, so get back," I said.

"He's making a list of the best-looking boys in the school," Cody, our star guard, said. "The winner gets to take him to the prom."

Billy's face tightened up but his boys started to laugh. He turned and gave them dirty looks. Then he turned to me and pointed his finger toward my face.

"You and me," he said. "You and me."

Then he left. His boys went with him.

"He doesn't know if he should try you or not," Cody said. "You're six feet with them wild dreads and stuff. You're hard to figure."

Good.

I wondered what would happen if Billy and his crew jumped me. I knew I could depend on Kambui and Cody. I thought of some of the other black dudes and about the Genius Gangstas. They were a bunch of guys who felt funny about being smart and needed a way of showing they were still down with the streets. But they were smart and they knew it and didn't want to give up being bright. So when Phat Tony, their bulgy leader, starting calling them the Genius Gangstas, they all went for it big-time. Maybe they would show if we got into a knockdown session with Billy's crew.

After practice I went home and thought I had forgotten about the whole thing, but our neighbor Mr. Albert was sitting on the stoop working out some checker moves on a ratty old board when I passed him by.

"Don't say hello, Zander!" he called after me.

"Hey, Mr. Albert," I said. "How's it going?"

"It's going good with me," he said, looking up from the checkerboard. "You're the one walking and talking to yourself. Your face is going a mile a minute and ain't a word coming out your mouth. What you thinking about so hard?"

"I've got a little situation going on in school," I said. "We're studying the Civil War and some of the students are making some remarks that make the black kids feel bad. It's nothing, really."

"That's why you walking down the street talking to yourself?" Mr. Albert asked, "because the situation ain't nothing? Let me tell you something, Zander. People start making remarks and causing trouble because it makes them feel good and it makes them feel special. And you know something? Trouble is like a party. When it don't cost you nothing to start you can bet somebody is going to start it."

"I guess so," I said.

"You guess so?" Mr. Albert looked up at me. "You can take that down to the bank and put it on deposit."

"Then I got to make it cost something," I said.

"But you got to have a win in it, too." Mr. Albert lowered his voice. "These young people going around this neighborhood fighting and killing each other up for mess that ain't got no win in it just drives me crazy."

"They're getting violent, and there's no win in it for them," I said.

"Amen, brother," Mr. Albert said, looking back down at his checkerboard. "Amen!"

I went upstairs, put on some shorts, and started doing deep knee bends and wondering what I looked like to Mr. Albert when he said I was talking to myself.

First I did fifty deep knee bends, then I did some push-ups and thought about how many push-ups Billy Stroud could do. Then I forced myself to stop thinking about Billy. Almost. Then Ashley called.

"Zander, I feel so terrible," she said. "I really do because I know that Alvin was using *The Palette* to make things terrible between the whites and the blacks. I'm really sorry."

"So, if you're the editor, you don't have to publish those things, right?" I said.

"Alvin is saying that you are trying to stop his freedom of speech. And I know that everybody should be able to speak, even if what they are saying is not what we want to hear," Ashley said. "And you know, my grandfather was an editor in the old Czechoslovakia. He published some stories that the government did not want printed and they came and beat him up and put him in jail for seven years. But that was the thing he was most proud of in his entire life. I want to be like him, to publish all sides of the truth."

What Ashley was saying was true, but sometimes something just being true wasn't very useful. It was like having a doctor tell you that the bone you thought was broken really was.

"Your grandfather must have been really brave," I said.

"He was," Ashley said in a soft voice. "But what is happening now is very embarrassing to me."

I told Ashley that everything was cool between me and her and that I would handle Alvin.

"The Cruisers should publish a rebuttal," she said. "Tell your side of the story. I'll publish it."

I told her I would think about it. I liked the way Ashley ran *The Palette*. She was really fair and always checked her facts before printing them, but she was conservative and said that *The Cruiser* was a "little on the wild side." I liked that.

I heard the key in the door. Mom.

She came in, took off her coat, threw it on the couch, then held her hands up for me to hold a minute. I watched her as she turned away for a few seconds, then whirled around with her hand on her hip and with this big smile on.

"Have you been trying to sell your time-share property for months without success? Are you ready for some action? Call 555-9495 today! Ta-dah!"

"That's good," I said.

"But it's only on cable," Mom said. "Starvation scale. Oh, yes, Marc wants to know if you want to play ball this weekend. How did school go today?"

"Not so good," I said. "Everybody's on my case. We're doing this Civil War thing —"

"Oh, yes, Kambui's grandmother called. Something about you starting a gang."

"Peacekeepers," I said. "We're supposed to be *preventing* the Civil War but we got into a fight with this group that calls itself the Sons of the Confederacy, and —"

"Real fight or fake fight?"

"Sort of both, because —"

"Can't be. It's either got to be real or not real," Mom said. "And why are you starting a gang?"

"I'm not starting a — we're just the opposite," I said. "We're peacekeepers."

"That's good," she said. "You want to make hamburgers, we've got some frozen patties, or you want to go out and get some Chinese food? I've got the money."

We went out for Chinese food and all the time she was telling me why she should play the role that Marc was trying to get for her. It was like the time she spent an entire Saturday morning telling me why we shouldn't be ashamed of our bodies and ended up with showing me a picture of herself in a fashion magazine wearing a bikini. It was okay with me because the magazine cost over nine dollars so I knew none of my friends would see it.

"So you think you shouldn't be in this film?" I asked her. We had ordered shrimp chop suey but they had put mushrooms in it and I was taking them out of mine.

"I just think some people aren't going to like the images of black people in the movie," Mom said. "They won't understand that it's supposed to be funny."

"Some guys in school are making jokes about slavery and saying it's funny," I said. "Maybe some things just aren't funny."

"Well, there was a lawyer at the studio I went to today," Mom said. "He said that if my income was good and I wasn't doing anything indecent that the court probably wouldn't take custody away from me."

"He say anything about how *I* was feeling?"

"Just that the courts would decide what was in your best interest," Mom said. "But it would help if you made it clear you're on my side."

"Okay."

"You are on my side, right?"

"Yeah."

"I heard they have snakes in Seattle, anyway."

THE CRUISER

THE LONDON ANTI-SLAVERY CONFERENCE
OF 1840 OR, FREEDOM IS A TRICKY SUCKER
By Zander Scott and Bobbi McCall

In 1840 there was a call put out by British abolitionists to have a conference in London. The
purpose of the conference was to make public
the evils of slavery and to plan ways of ending it
throughout the world. Words like "equality,"
"brotherhood," and "liberty" rang out in homes
and auditoriums as the passionate attendees
began to arrive. But when the American delega-
tion arrived there was an instant uproar. The
Americans included people like Lucretia Mott
and 25-year-old Elizabeth Cady Stanton. The
British were appalled. When they spoke of "equality" and "liberty" they didn't mean women.

The British abolitionists decided that their
usual way of conducting business changed the

meaning of the word "equality," and when they spoke of "full rights" for everyone they really meant rights for everyone who has a penis.

The Sons of the Confederacy speak of "freedom of speech" when they publish their nasty little items in *The Palette* or now in *The Charleston Courier.* But what they really mean is the freedom to say anything they want without being responsible for their statements.

Just as it is generally accepted that shouting "fire" in a crowded theater when in fact there is no fire is not acceptable, and that slander is not acceptable, we should also hold the Sons of the Confederacy accountable for their unacceptable messages.

The British abolitionists got away with it in 1840 by making the women who attended sit behind a curtain. We don't sit behind curtains today!

CHAPTER SIX

Throw in a Beat Box and You Got AutoDad

Friday morning. I came out to breakfast and Mom was on the phone. She had her head back with slices of cucumber on her eyelids.

"No, I can't have lunch with you tomorrow," she said as the cucumber slices came off and she pointed toward the orange juice. "I'm busy. And beside, isn't it time you and Zander had lunch? I mean, don't you have some man-to-man stuff to talk about?"

I poured her some orange juice, wondering who she was talking to.

"He's busy tonight," she said. "And anyway, he doesn't eat in fast-food restaurants. Didn't you know that?"

She put her hand over the telephone and mouthed the words "your father."

"Okay, tomorrow, then. No, don't come here," she said. "Where do you want to meet Zander and at what time? On 135th Street? No, it burned down. The restaurant in Harlem Hospital? Just a minute."

Mom covered the phone with her hand again.

"Your father's in town," she said. "He wants to have lunch with you tomorrow. He's flying back to Seattle Sunday evening. Is one o'clock okay?"

"Yeah, I guess."

She made arrangements for us to meet at the hospital cafeteria, which was way good because they had great burgers and okay fries. All the time she was talking to him she was looking at me. She was trying to keep her calm on, but her hands were actually shaking.

I wanted to say something smart to her, but I didn't know what, so I just kept quiet.

Life with Mom was good. It was interesting but it wasn't always easy. Sometimes we didn't have money and sometimes I got mad at her because of it. Sometimes, I knew, she got mad at herself.

Mom was in a kissing mood but I got out of most of it. I asked her was she going to see my father this weekend and she said no, that she was too busy. His being in New York always got her upset so it was okay with me.

"I don't want you to be against your father," she said.

"Not even a little?" I asked.

She smiled. We were cool that way.

All day in school I thought about meeting up with my father. Mom said he was trying too hard to be a good father.

"He wants to be too many good things," she went on. "He wanted to be a good husband, a good American, a good weatherman. He even wanted to make perfect eggs Benedict. Do you know what that is?"

"Yeah, Mom, it's Da Vinci Academy for the Gifted," I said. "Not the Drifted. It's when they make funky eggs and put them on English muffins."

"Well, one time he made them and they came out really crappy, I mean *seriously* crappy, and I called them eggs Benedict Arnold and he was hurt," she said. "He was really hurt."

I thought he was trying, too, but Mom was right. He did things by the book even if you weren't on the same page. It was like Jay-Z talking about Auto-Tune. You could screech away and still come close to the right notes but it still didn't make it.

Saturday came and I walked downtown.

"Hey, Zander! What you up to these days?" Mr. Watson, who lived on my block, was the cook at the restaurant in Harlem Hospital.

"Nothing much," I said. "Having lunch with my father."

"That's good," Mr. Watson said. "Especially if he's paying. Order the steak."

"I don't want the steak," I said.

I found a booth facing the door and parked in it. I knew my father was going to get there right on time. The dude was never late. I just hoped he didn't bring me a stupid present that I was supposed to ooh and aah over.

"Alexander!" *Bam!* Right on time. "You're looking good!" My father had on his best smile as he slid into the booth. Donald Scott, weatherman, had on a brown sport jacket, blue shirt, and dark slacks. I had on my New York Knicks sweatshirt.

"How you doing?" I asked.

"Couldn't be better," he said. "You order yet?"

"No," I said.

"Hey, guy, brought you something," he said, reaching into his pocket. "It's a rhyming dictionary."

I didn't know what he expected me to do with it but I took it from him and opened it up. It was kind of embarrassing because I knew I didn't want it but I didn't want to tell him that.

"'Case you're thinking up a rap while you're on the A train," he said, "and needed some rhymes."

That was so lame.

"Yeah, okay."

"So what's going on?"

"Nothing much," I said.

"Your mother tells me that you're studying the Civil War," he said, picking up the menu to figure out what salad he was going to order. "That's good stuff, the Civil War. Important American history. Few people understand that many of the issues we face today, the balance of powers between the federal government and the states, were hammered out in that bloody conflict."

"If you say so."

We sat there for a while and he ran through his checklist of the things to say to your kid when you live on the West Coast and your kid lives on the East Coast. How pretty the girls were on the East Coast, how boating was a favorite sport in the Seattle area, and how many more people drove sports cars in Washington.

"More open highway," he said. "Not in the SeaTac region itself but on the outskirts, as you head toward Mount Rainier. You got the pictures of Mount Rainier I sent you. Your mother said you liked them."

He even started talking about how well the Seattle SuperSonics were going to do.

"The SuperSonics suck," I said.

He looked a little hurt when I said that and I felt bad, but I didn't take it back.

It was funny, because being around him always made me mad, but I wanted to be around him more. It made me mad because he was always trying too hard and I wished he wouldn't. I wished he could just chill out and be whoever he was.

"So, tell me about the Civil War," he said, still trying.

"It was a war, the Union won, end of story," I said.

"Sometimes things are more complex than that," he said. "Even with the weather. A rainy day is good weather for an umbrella salesman but bad weather for a lifeguard. It's a matter of perspective."

"Unless you're a cloud," I said. "Then your life is over."

"That's . . . very creative," my father said. "But you need to see what the people were thinking were their reasons for the war, too."

He always mumbled when he wasn't sure of himself. In a way I liked that about him. And what I said about the cloud wasn't creative. It was stupid and we both knew it but there we were. I was on the East Coast and he was on the West.

He ordered a tuna salad platter and I ordered a burger deluxe.

"By the way," he said, holding up his fork with a piece of tomato on the end of it, "I called your school about two weeks ago. Just thought I'd see how you were doing."

"Why didn't you ask me?" I said. "Or Mom."

"Well, sometimes it's good for the school to know that both parents are interested," he said. The tomato disappeared into his mouth.

"And what did the school say?" I asked.

"Said that you were among the brightest and the best," he said. He pronounced his *T*'s like he was announcing something. "But, somehow, your grades don't reflect that."

"I'm working on that," I said.

"I'm wondering if you might be better off in a school in the Seattle area," he said. "There are some great schools in the U district."

"U district?"

"University district," he said. "Lots of kids whose parents teach at the University of Washington or some of the other schools. Lots of competition. Think you could stand being around a lot of brainy young people?"

"Don't want to go to no Seattle," I said.

"You know, Alexander . . ." He had his fingers together in front of his nose as if he was going to say something deep. "Sometimes we don't always know what's best for us. You only get one chance at a good education and you have to take advantage of it. If you're not doing well living here in Harlem then you have an obligation to yourself to be someplace else."

"Mom is here in Harlem," I said.

"Your education is not about your mother and it's not about me, frankly," he said. "It's about you and your chances in life."

"You got Mom really upset when you sent that thing — the subpoena," I said. "Why you have to do that?"

"Because I care for you and I want answers, not promises," he said. "As I said, it's not about me or your mother. And I didn't send it as just a guy who lives an awfully long way from a son he loves very much. I sent it as a father who would just hate to see that son throwing away his talent because he's not being closely supervised. Did I tell you that Carrie is a teacher? She could really help you get back on track."

"Who's Carrie?"

"Oh, uh, your stepmother," he said. "You didn't remember her name?"

Her name was Carolyn and I did remember it. I also remembered what she looked like because he sent me a photograph of her. She was young looking with a round face and reddish-brown hair. Mom and I drew a mustache on her before we threw the photograph away.

"I'm not going to Seattle," I said.

"We'll explore all of our options," he said.

He switched the conversation to basketball and asked me what position I was playing. I told him I was playing forward and he said I would be tall enough soon to play center.

"I don't want to play center," I said.

We didn't talk much after that and I thought he was glad when the lunch was over. He asked me if I needed cab money to get home and I told him I was going to walk.

"I'm taking a cab downtown — corporate offices. I'll drop you off first uptown," he said, standing on the sidewalk.

"I'm walking."

We did our firm handshake bit and I watched as he hailed a cab and started downtown.

I wished things were different, that he and Mom were together. But they weren't, and that was the way it was. I thought about LaShonda. Her parents had been really young when they left her with an aunt one day and just never come back. At least I was living with Mom and knew my father was around someplace. Maybe if I was around him more I wouldn't feel I had to put him down so much.

When I got to 145th Street there were police cars in front of the house. The cops had three teenagers lying across the hood of a patrol car. There was a crowd of people, mostly kids and women, standing around.

"I just seen it there!" one of the teenagers was yelling. "I didn't even touch it."

I saw Mr. Albert standing a little way off and went over to him.

"What's happened?" I asked.

"Them boys were walking down the street and a cop car pulled up on them real sudden like," Mr. Albert said. "When they saw the cops getting out their car they looked like they wanted to run but the cops were on them too quick. The police found a paper bag with some dope in it and they all swearing it don't belong to none of them."

"Drugs ain't even about me," one of the kids was yelling. I saw his hands were cuffed behind him. "I ain't no crackhead."

"I hate drugs, man!" one of the other kids said.

The cops made the people watching move back onto the other sidewalk or down the street.

"Just another day on the streets," Mr. Albert said. "Three more young men get to ride in the backseat of a police car."

"They're saying they don't like drugs," I said. "Maybe they're innocent."

"Could be," Mr. Albert said. "And maybe they hate drugs and maybe they love drugs but it don't make no never mind. The police are saying that if you got it you own it. They got the drugs and now they got to own it and pay the consequences. That's the way life is. They should have thought about what they had when they were bopping down the street with it."

Mr. Albert was right. They put them all in the patrol car and soon they were headed downtown to the 135th Street police station.

When I got home, Mom was there and she asked me how things went with my father.

"Bad," I said.

"Why?" She put down the papers she was looking at and sat down at the table.

"Mostly because he was trying to be supercool and I was busy being a jerk," I said.

She laughed at that and then I laughed and it was good. She said maybe we should send my father an apology.

We both said "nahh!" together.

One Story — Sad, then Not Sad, then Sad Again
From LaShonda Powell's Diary

Okay, first the sad part. I'm still living at St. Francis, which is a group home for kids who either don't have no folks or their folks don't have them. Same difference. My moms died when she was sixteen and I really don't know much about her except she had had me and my brother by then. My father is out there in the Great Somewhere, and peace to him. End of sad part.

Here comes the Not Sad part. Last week I met a woman who said she had known my mother back in the day. She said she still had her yearbook from Wadleigh and that I could have it if I wanted it. She didn't have any other real stuff about my moms so I went and picked up the yearbook. Inside the yearbook, near the back, I found my mother's report card. There were a lot of remarks on it about her poor attendance record and "difficult" home life. But then I scoped the chick's grades and they were smoking! She had straight A's in everything except Social Studies and she copped a B+ in that. You always hear about people hoping their kids do better than they did. If you can get next to that you can get next to how I feel knowing my mom did better than me when everybody I know was badmouthing her as a druggie who OD'd on a rooftop. I was glad to find her report card.

Now for the sad part again. I wish I had gone to school with her. I just know we could have hung out and been friends. We would have been homegirls and I would have been watching her back 24/7. Whatever she needed I could have got it for her, because that's the kind of girl I am and she would have done the same for me. Word.

CHAPTER SEVEN
Sometimes You Can't Get an Answer
Because the Question Didn't Show Up

Me, Bobbi, Cody, and Kambui were in the media center looking up the causes for the Civil War. Miss LoBretto got all excited and started giving us a bunch of resources when all we wanted was a short, easy list. But we did get to the Declarations of Causes of Secession. The first states that broke away from the Union had their reasons and they were all about the differences between their states and the non-slave states and what rights they had under the Constitution. It was confusing and Bobbi loved it.

"It's like thinking about infinite number possibilities," she said, wiggling in her seat the way she does when she's pleased with herself. "Suppose you designed a computer that could multiply the number one by itself an infinite number of times —"

"It would still always be one," Cody said.

"Right, and it would be the same if you divided one by itself," Bobbi said. She was delighted with herself. "Isn't that cool?"

"No, it's not," I said. "I don't even know what you're talking about."

"Well, that's what it's all about with math," Bobbi said. "You have to get in there and figure out all the relationships between the numbers and what they mean. It's a lot clearer than using words."

I was beginning to see that.

All the reasons given for the causes of the Civil War seemed flaky to me because none of them included any feelings that black people had or even if it was right to have slaves in the first place. In a way Alvin and the Sons were tiptoeing around the same as the people had before the war broke out.

The next day Cody sent me a text message saying he had been grounded for life for supporting the Cruisers. Bobbi sent a message that Alvin had said in his Hip Baller Blog that she was secretly Puerto Rican.

if i wz i wd h'ook ↑ w/the D man

The D man was Demetrius Brown, whose parents were from Cuba, and I didn't even know Bobbi had eyes for him but I did know that we were getting next to Alvin.

Me and Kambui took our bikes to school on Monday. It was a short trip but it was fun. Kambui had painted his helmet black and put stars all over it, which made it look stupid, but I didn't mention it.

I was feeling confident when I got to school because I thought that the Cruisers were deep into the game and working out okay. Then I saw some of Alvin's boys gathered in the hallway around Mr. Culpepper. One of them pointed me out when I came in and Mr. Culpepper turned and took a look at me.

That's when my brain flashed a message. Memo to self: Get with the Cruisers and meet Mr. Culpepper at lunchtime.

Culpepper made an exception to his rule about writing a note to get into see him, so by the afternoon, when we got to his office, I was feeling pretty much okay. Ashley was looking worried, while all the time Alvin was acting like the world really belonged to him and we were just renting space or something. Bobbi, Kambui, and LaShonda were looking down at their feet.

"My father said that the Civil War was about a lot of issues," Alvin said. "He even wrote an article about it for a magazine. He said that slavery was only one issue and even that wasn't just about race."

"One of the things we are not going to do from now on," Mr. Culpepper said in his Sunday morning holier-than-thou voice, "is accuse someone of being racist unless we can absolutely prove it. Is that understood by every-one here?"

"If only black people were slaves," I asked, "why isn't that about race?"

"Well, that's not the point, is it?" Mr. Culpepper said. "You're talking about events that happened a hundred and fifty years ago. You can't say that Alvin is a racist because he is merely reenacting those days."

"And when the Confederate states seceded they didn't talk about race," I said. "They were talking about property rights. So if you call slaves property how come it's not about race?"

"It's a very complex issue, Mr. Scott," Mr. Culpepper said. "The states of the Confederacy were quoting the Constitution when they claimed your — the slaves — as property. That might be too complex for eighth-graders."

Okay, now I was seeing it. Mr. Culpepper was talking about slavery being too complex and too hard for eighth-graders to think about. It didn't seem that hard to me — it was either right or wrong. I didn't see why that was complex. Then I thought about what Mr. Albert had said about the teenagers the police had on the ground. Maybe race was more like drugs than people thought. When they could use race it was good, but nobody wanted to own it when they got caught using it.

"So how important is it for me to be in a movie?" Mom, as usual, had the phone on speaker and was combing out her hair as she talked to Marc. "And how important is it to you to get the fifteen percent?"

"Melba, it's your career, not mine." Marc's voice came over the speaker. "I'm just telling you that I think the exposure will be good for you."

"I'll think about it," Mom said.

"That's what you said last week," Marc replied.

"And I did," Mom said. "I really did."

Marc did some cursing, then hung up.

"How come you don't want to be in the movie?" I asked.

"Well, it could be a good movie," Mom said. "But it could really be a bust. Have you ever seen *Gone with the Wind*?"

"Why would I want to see that old flick?"

"Okay, so I guess you haven't seen it. It was about this white girl on a plantation in Georgia at the beginning of the Civil War. She's spoiled and bratty and kind of mindless. The first guy she was going to marry dropped her, and then she meets this cool guy played by Clark Gable and she falls for him big-time but he only partway falls for her. Anyway, she's got this black maid and there are plenty of black people in the movie. Hattie McDaniel won an Oscar for best supporting actress."

"She was black, right?"

"Right. So then they were having the war and all these Southern boys were marching up and down and acting like they were going off to a picnic and looking pretty good in their uniforms. The war went on for most of the movie and ended up with the burning of Atlanta."

"They talked about race a lot?"

"Nope. They just skipped around it and talked about Southern honor and protecting the South, that kind of thing," Mom said. She was wearing a bright red blouse and was trying on a yellow scarf, holding it against the blouse to see how the colors matched. "They didn't even talk about slaves from what I remember about the movie."

"So Hattie McDaniel was free?"

"No, they just didn't talk about her being a slave." Mom was laying out clothes on the bed. "I guess the producers didn't want the movie to be controversial."

"But she was a slave?" I asked again.

"Yes. They want me to play her part in this satirical movie," Mom said. "Do you know what satirical means?"

"Sure I know what it means," I said. "It's when being funny makes a point."

"Okay, but the problem is that sometimes these movies start out to be satire and then end up just plain silly. I don't want to be running around with a bandanna around my head looking stupid. Besides, the movie is supposed to show how racist the story was and you can't show anything about racism if it's all about joking around."

"If you have so many bad feelings about the movie why are you thinking about doing it?" I asked.

"Because I also have bad feelings about taking money from your father and sometimes struggling to make a living for us," she said.

"Complex, huh?"

"I think it is," Mom said. "Do you think I look good in red?"

"No."

"I do, too," she said.

THE CRUISER

Dear Miss McDaniel,

I am glad you won an Oscar for your role in *Gone with the Wind* but I wish that at least one time you had turned to the camera and said, "I am a slave." I know that they would have probably cut that out of the movie or even have taken you out of the movie altogether. But the problem I'm having is that when you don't name something you can't deal with it unless everybody is agreeing to it.

Some people, a lot of people, really, think they can get away with putting people down just by changing the names they use. When somebody says that I'm from the inner city they are not talking about where I live, but they are saying

75

that I'm part of an urban scene they really don't respect. I have never heard anybody say, "Oh, he's really cool because he lives in the inner city."

My mother said that you weren't running around acting stupid in the movie and that was good. But if you were somebody's slave you should have said that, too. Then they could make up their mind if they liked the person who kept you in slavery. I guess you needed the money and it's hard getting a good role in the movies. But from what I have heard about the movie just about everybody was let off the hook about who they really were.

None of this would matter if we weren't dealing with race today. Some people, like Mr. Culpepper in our school, say that we are dealing with other issues. But if you see kids laughing and smirking and making little

"jokes" like offering somebody up for sale (somebody who would punch him out!), you would know
better.

Your friend,

Zander

CHAPTER EIGHT
Watch Brer McRabbit Shake that Thing

Cody called. Kelly Bena, who plays cello in the school band, saw Alvin's new blog post and texted LaShonda, who left a message on Cody's Facebook page. Alvin had volunteered to hand out sandwiches to homeless people at a shelter near Marcus Garvey Park in Harlem. He said he wanted to get himself involved in the swim of things, whatever that meant.

"He said he had told Ashley but didn't think she would print it in *The Palette*," Cody said.

Okay, so Alvin was working Ashley. He knew she would print the story about him feeding homeless people in Harlem.

I needed to talk to somebody. I was going to call Kambui but he was still in his "let's get tough" mode. LaShonda was leaning his way, too, and so I called Bobbi.

"Yo, Bobbi, how come everybody is playing a game with us but nobody's standing still long enough for us to get on their case?" I said. "Alvin was running his little Confederacy thing big-time and now he's about feeding homeless people in Harlem."

"Zander, people can be about more than one thing," Bobbi said. "Sometimes when you see the old movies about the South and you see all the people dressed up like ladies and gentlemen it's really nice. The way they have it in movies, with all the black people taking off their hats and smiling like they didn't know they were slaves, it's kind of romantic and pretty. Sort of like a reality show in reverse."

"That's exactly what it's like," I said. "Those reality shows where everybody is acting like they're getting mad at each other or working together and all the time you know there's a bunch of cameras about ten feet away from them."

"I'd like to be on a reality show," Bobbi said. "I think it would be fun. Nothing in the woods, though. They should have one called *Survival at the Mall*. What do you think?"

"I think that's stupid, but if they get one, I'll put your name in for it," I said.

When I hung up from Bobbi, I was seeing things clearer. People were doing their little dirt but it was like a reality show they could just back away from. They didn't have to own anything. Like my father saying it wasn't about him and his new wife, it was about me. And the kid on the patrol car saying that the dope the police found wasn't his. But all the cops had to do was to take them downtown and say they saw them with it and that would be it. They owned it.

I finished the last pages of *A Raisin in the Sun*, then looked up the synopsis on the Net to see if they agreed with me. They did but they thought it was a dynamite play and I thought it wasn't all that hot.

Then I read the Declarations of Causes of Secession of some of the seceding states that Mr. Siegfried had assigned us and read them over again. The states talked about property and the Constitution, but none of them talked about how the slaves felt or holding human beings against their will. Alvin wasn't talking about it, either, and I needed to change that.

THE CRUISER

ROBBY MCRABBIT GETS INTO THE

SWIM OF THINGS: A STORY

By LaShonda Powell

Ain't none of the bears in Vinci Woods liked Robby McRabbit. Robby was a nasty little rabbit that was always talking trash to the bears.

"All y'all bears got stink breaths and big feet!" he said.

Them bears used to look at Robby McRabbit, and when they did they were mean mugging him from the tip of his pointy ears to his nasty little toes.

"Them feet of yours would sure look good on a key chain!" Bo Bear called out.

Robby McRabbit didn't care. He would just turn his little fluffy tail toward the bears and give it a little shake-shake and grin because he was satisfied being his nasty self.

But one Saturday Robby McRabbit was sitting in the woods all by himself. He was listening to the laughing going on from the picnic that the bears held each weekend.

"I sure would like to have something good to eat," he said.

He peeped through the tall leaves and saw the bears doing the Swim, a new dance that one of the bears had learned in Memphis, Tennessee. All the bears were doing it and having a nice time.

The Swim started off with the bears just moving their hips. Then they started moving their stomachs in and out, and finally they got their whole bodies going left and right and 'round and 'round while their arms made a motion that looked like they was swimming. *Ummmm-um!* It sure looked good to Robby McRabbit.

Robby McRabbit thought about it and thought he could learn that dance. It didn't look like much and he already had the moves down by practicing in front of a mirror.

He practiced by himself for a whole week and then went over to where the bears lived.

"Look," he said, "I can do the Swim."

He started with his hips moving and then his stomach and then he got his arms going just right. Or that's what he thought, anyway.

"You ain't doing it right," Bo Bear said. "Get in the line and we'll show you how to do it."

All the bears lined up and they started moving their hips. When all of them got the hips going they started moving their stomachs in and out. When they got that down they started moving their arms like they was swimming and also started moving around in a circle.

Robby McRabbit was at the end of the line, right behind a lady bear with a big behind. He followed her and he was really getting down.

"You ain't moving your arms right," Bo Bear said. "You got to do it like I do it."

Robby McRabbit didn't say nothing. He just watched Bo Bear, making sure that he didn't get up into his face too much because he had stink breath just the way Robby McRabbit knew he would.

"Rabbits don't swim like bears," Robby McRabbit said. "I do the Swim different than you do."

"You got to learn how we do it if you want to hang out with us," Bo Bear said. "Get on in the water."

The bears had made them a round pool just big enough for two bears to get into. Robby McRabbit didn't want to learn to swim like no bear but he wanted to hang out and party with them. He jumped into the pool and old Bo Bear turned up the music.

The sounds were on the money and the beat was deep. Robby McRabbit started moving his hips and was looking good but he started to sink.

"Throw me a life preserver!" he cried.

All the bears threw in life preservers. Robby McRabbit thought the bears were stupid because they were throwing in celery and onions and you couldn't hang on to no celery or no onion.

"I'm fixing to drown up in here!" Robby McRabbit called out.

"That's 'cause the water is too cold to swim in!" said Bo Bear, and he started a fire under the pool.

When the water got a little warmer it made Robby McRabbit feel good and he started moving better.

"I think I'm getting it!" he said, noticing that the water was getting a little too warm.

After a while the water got really hot and

Robby McRabbit was jumping around and hollering, but it was too late. He was soon Robby McRabbit stew and the hit of the picnic.

After all the dancing and the eating was over Bo Bear sat with his friends drinking Kool-Aid and listening to some jams.

"Rabbits are good to have at picnics," he said. "But don't they make your breath stink?"

He got an "Amen" behind that.

CHAPTER NINE
The Attack on Fort Sumter!

In the lunchroom. The service counter had peas, green beans, some nasty-looking spinach, rice, something that looked yellow and round, spaghetti, chicken tenders, fish sticks, chilled pears, and cookies. I settled on the fish sticks and spaghetti. I looked around and saw LaShonda and Bobbi sitting together and went over.

"Yo, what you doing?" I asked LaShonda.

"She's painting the first ten prime numbers on my fingernails," Bobbi said. "I would have her paint the next ten on my toenails but they're too small."

"You don't have any toenails," LaShonda said, holding up her nail polish. "You have toenails on your big toes but your other nails are too small to be called real nails. They're just like tiny spots on top of your feet."

"That is seriously stupid," I said.

"What are you eating?" Bobbi pointed to my plate.

"Fish sticks and spaghetti," I answered.

"That doesn't look like a fish to me," Bobbi said. "It doesn't have a tail, it doesn't have eyes, and it's rectangular. If you threw it in the water, it wouldn't swim, and if you walked down the street it wouldn't follow you home. And I've never heard of a fish called 'stick.' And now you're going to put it in your mouth and eat it. Now *that's* weird, Zander."

"It looked better than the chicken tenders," I said.

BLAM! BLAM!

I was trying to think of something else to say when we heard the noise coming from the other side of the lunchroom. Everything got quiet for a second and then it came again.

BLAM!

I looked over the table and saw kids clearing out from near the window.

"Come on, punk!" It was Alvin McCraney pulling off his shirt. "Bring it! Bring it!"

He was facing off with Kambui about four feet from the far wall.

I started across the floor as fast as I could. I didn't want Kambui getting into any fights in the lunchroom. I was almost to them when I saw something out of the corner of my eye. It was a body coming toward me.

I couldn't tell who it was but then I saw another blur as two guys clashed, knocking a girl down as their bodies crashed onto a table. I could see the second body. It was Cody.

I turned back to where Alvin was still standing, his shirt half off and his face pale and twisted with anger. His mouth fell open as he saw Cody and Billy tangling big-time.

I got between Kambui and Alvin and held my hands up. From the corner of my eye I saw some of Alvin's friends move behind him. It looked like the war was about to begin.

"What's going on here?" A man's voice. Then again, slower. "What is going on here?"

"Nothing." Alvin McCraney was putting his shirt back on.

"Cody?!" Mr. Culpepper watched as Cody and Billy untangled themselves.

"Nothing, sir," Cody said.

"Your father would not appreciate your fighting in the lunchroom, Cody," Mr. Culpepper said. He was puffed up so that his neck looked bigger than his head.

"No fight, sir," Cody said.

"Okay, then," Mr. Culpepper said. "Let's see if you gentlemen can live up to the title."

He looked around again and then walked away. I knew if it had been anyone except Cody there would have been a lot more screaming and taking down of names. Cody's father worked in the school and Mr. Culpepper didn't want to make trouble for him. I watched as Alvin and some of his guys got together and shot some dirty looks our way before leaving the lunchroom together.

"I don't know if they make jerks in grades," Cody said, standing near me, "but if they do, then Billy Stroud is class A all the way. He was coming at you like a freight train."

"Thanks, man," I said.

"No problemo," Cody said.

I went over to Kambui and saw that he was steaming mad.

A girl named Zhade Hopkins, Shantese's sister, was with him and I asked her to tell LaShonda and Bobbi to meet us in the media center. Kambui had a thing for Zhade. He'd been trying to get a date with her for over a year.

"If you guys get into it don't use any guns," Zhade said. "It ain't worth it."

The word was on the street.

"We need to get some brothers together and just get busy with the Sons of the Confederacy and anybody else who needs to get his head whipped," Kambui said, looking me down. We were meeting in the media center and Kambui had brought the Jackson brothers and Phat Tony from the Genius Gangstas to the meeting. "I'm dealing on my own because you're acting like you're scared of them."

"I'm not scared of anybody," I said. "But if we're going to war you need to show me the win you found. If there's going to be a fight there's got to be a win in it somewhere. Show me what you got."

"One of Alvin's dudes came up to me in Social Studies and said if I picked enough cotton he would let me sit on the front porch with him in the evening," LaShonda said. "I told him if he needed any cotton picked he'd better tell his mama to pick it. Making him keep his mouth shut is a win for me."

"And Alvin was up in my face in the lunchroom," Kambui said. "He's moved the set from his little jokes to jumping bad because he knows you're too scared to fight."

"The civil rights movement wasn't about fighting," I said. "Martin Luther King, Jr., wasn't about fighting."

"No, but he had some righteous brothers in the streets who were ready to get down if they had to," Kambui said. "And Frederick Douglass was down for peace but he still told Abraham Lincoln that the Union needed to get some black soldiers involved in the Civil War. Yo, man, if it was good enough for Frederick Douglass, it's good enough for me."

"I think Zander is running shy," LaShonda said. "He definitely doesn't look like he's ready for no serious throw down."

"I think we should remain true to our role as peacekeepers," Bobbi said. "And that's not about fighting."

"Bobbi McCall, how are you going to fix your mouth to say that when you're not black?" LaShonda asked. "It doesn't affect you the way it does us."

"LaShonda, I may not be as dark as you" — Bobbi got both hands up on her hips — "but I'm every bit as human as you are. If you're putting down human beings, then you're putting me down, too."

"Anybody that paints their nails with the prime numbers is not as human as I am," LaShonda said. "You may be smart but you are freaky."

"Yeah, well, that, too, LaShonda," Bobbi said, checking out her nails. "But that doesn't move me away from what I'm feeling about this."

"Alvin's walking around with bodyguards now," Kambui said. "He's been hanging out with some of the big guys in the school. I think they're just looking for a fight."

"Yeah, but isn't that the way all wars get started?" I asked. "The textbook said that most of the people in the South didn't have slaves but got caught up in the idea they were fighting for their states or for their homes. I think they forgot about why they were fighting and just got on with it."

"Whatever!" Kambui was on his feet. "The bottom line is that he's walking around with his ha-ha on and it's us that he's goofing on. It might not bother you because you're not rolling with the people, but it bothers me."

"And having these dudes up in my face is messing with my mind," LaShonda said. "They're fingerpicking on my *last* nerve and making me feel four kinds of stupid because I ain't got no comeback!"

"Okay, if I can get Alvin and his crew to the table and make them own what they're running, will you hang with me?" I asked.

"How are you going to do that?" Kambui rolled his eyes toward me.

"They don't want to take credit for what they're saying," I said. "They want to make it light stuff and, like you're saying, they're blowing themselves up and thinking they can push up on us. Okay, suppose we give them credit and give them exactly what they want. Suppose we start agreeing with what they're saying but put it up front so they can't get around it?"

"Zander, are your mouth and brain on the same page? What are you talking about?" LaShonda's voice went up about four notes.

"He's punking out," Kambui said.

"I'm not punking out," I said. "I just think if we make the Sons of the Confederacy responsible for what they're saying and doing we'll have something going on that we can deal with."

"So what's your plan?" Bobbi asked.

It wasn't a whole plan but I didn't want to say that. It was like a little bit of *Gone with the Wind*, a little bit of real history and some of that luck Mr. Culpepper said we were going to need.

"Look, in the movie *Gone with the Wind* they had a bunch of black people on their plantation but they didn't call them slaves. They called them servants like they were just working there part-time or something," I said. "If they had signs around their necks that read 'Slave,' then the movie would have been different. Slavery was the name of the thing going on then, and we got to bring the name to this set. If LaShonda can work her Facebook connections and her IM circuits to let everybody know what we're doing, we might pull something off."

"Which is what?" LaShonda asked.

"We get all the blacks in the eighth grade to start acting like they're slaves and bowing and crossing the hall when they meet the white students."

"I'm not doing that," Kambui said. "No way. It's stupid, man. I'd rather go down swinging than lame my way through this crap."

"I don't think it's stupid, Kambui," Bobbi said. "I see where Zander's going. Say the teacher comes into the room and asks who took a book off the desk and everybody turns and looks at LaShonda —"

"Why does it have to be me?" LaShonda asked. "I don't take people's books."

"Right," I said. "But you'd have to answer the questions about it if we all acted as if you did."

"And we're supposed to be acting like slaves so that Alvin has to answer the questions about his attitude?" Kambui had his arms crossed.

"Not only Alvin," I answered. "But everybody who is saying it's just a freedom of speech thing and it's just a play thing and it's everything except what it really is, a lot of joking around that's making people feel bad."

"And suppose it doesn't work and they just keep on with their ha-ha attitude?" Kambui asked.

I looked over at him and took a deep breath. "This is Tuesday. We'll get it together for Thursday morning. I'll run off a broadside edition of *The Cruiser* tonight and we'll give that out tomorrow. Then, if the joint doesn't run by Friday afternoon I'll punch Alvin out at three o'clock," I said.

"I don't think you can beat Alvin," Kambui said. "But I'll run with it until Friday."

"If it don't work out I'll see what happens Friday," I said. "All I'm asking is that you work for me until then."

"Wait a minute, I just thought of something," Bobbi said. "You might have noticed something about me, folks. Like, I'm cute and white. What am I supposed to be doing when you're walking around acting like slaves?"

"What do you want to do?" I asked.

"She can hold the guns," Phat Tony said. "We can contact the Bloods, the Crips, and the Mexican Mafia and get them on our side of the ave."

"I just want to get with the program," Bobbi said. "Not get pushed to the side."

"Instead of us all acting, let's run with a visual," Kambui said. "We can have signs around our necks. Remember reading about the civil rights movement and the brothers carrying signs that read 'I Am a Man'? That's what I need to feel like, right now. A man."

Kambui's idea was good and I went with it. "Okay, how about us wearing signs that just say 'I Have Been Degraded'?" I said.

"Then I can be on board," Bobbi said. "It sounds like a plan to me."

I told everybody that I would make the signs up and

have them ready to wear. I knew I could run them off on our printer and then glue them down on some heavy oak tag.

The Jackson brothers, Kambui, and LaShonda left together and I knew they would be talking about me.

"You sure about this?" Bobbi asked.

"Yes," I said. "Don't you think it's going to work?"

"If I were you I'd bring some bandages to school Friday morning," she said.

The thing was that if it didn't work and I did fight Alvin it would be just enough to get me kicked out of Da Vinci. Maybe even all the way to Seattle.

THE CRUISER

The Da Vinci Cruisers, who were trying to make peace between the North and South factions and prevent the Civil War, have come to an agreement with the Sons of the Confederacy that slavery was not an issue because the feelings of black people don't matter. "You can say anything you want about black people," said Zander Scott. "We don't matter because, as Alvin McCraney has pointed out, we aren't civilized. So our feelings don't count." We therefore encourage all Da Vinci students and teachers to disrespect everything dealing with African Americans for the rest of the school year. We also offer the following resolution for the approval of all Da Vinci students: It does not matter that the Africans brought to America from 1619 to 1807 were degraded into a state of slavery and that they, and their descendants, can still be degraded today within the halls of Da Vinci Academy.

— The Cruisers

CHAPTER TEN
I've Been 'Buked and I've Been Scorned!

Mom has this thing she does with her teeth. First she flosses, then she brushes, then she uses this machine that sends water through her mouth. She's got great-looking teeth and wants me to do the same thing but I didn't think I wanted to go through all that. She's got another thing she can do, even with the water running and toothpaste foaming around her mouth. She can hear a telephone.

She made a signal for me that our phone was ringing and pushed me toward the living room. It was LaShonda.

"I thought you were running on empty but now I think you got something going on," she said.

"Like what?"

"I called about ten of the black kids I know and told them your plan and they were all over it!" I could hear the excitement in her voice. "You know, nobody was speaking out but now that you've got something they can run with they're coming around. How many signs did you make?"

"Twenty-five," I answered. "Then I ran out of ink because I did it in Photoshop on my ink-jet."

"Get some more ink," LaShonda said. "I got a feeling."

"There aren't that many black kids in the school," I said.

"Zander, word has spread — it's not just the black kids calling me," LaShonda said. "Get the ink!"

I told Mom what LaShonda said about what was happening, showed her the sign, and told her I needed to cop some printer juice. Her money wasn't that heavy but she gave what she had.

"Demonstrations always work," she said. "At least they let people know you're pissed off."

I hadn't thought of that, but it was something to tell the kids at school.

I got the ink and started making more signs. They measured eleven by seventeen on card stock and they looked good. The bold lettering took a lot of ink but the words really stood out. I looped the ends of the string and stapled them to the card stock so the signs could be hung around the neck. All in all there were nearly a hundred signs, although I didn't think I'd need half of them.

As I put the signs together I started telling myself not to be nervous. It was as if I was overhearing myself saying, "Calm down, Zander, calm down."

I really wanted the demonstration to be successful. Maybe I even needed it to work. LaShonda's call gave me confidence, but then I started thinking that maybe the message wasn't strong enough. Kambui and LaShonda had both said I was coming on too weak. It was clear that we were being degraded. Everyone knew that and, for a while, I wondered if I had enough ink to do the whole thing over with something stronger. But then I thought about the signs that the workers in Memphis carried that read "I Am a Man." People could see that the workers there were men, but the way they were being treated, as if they just had to do what they were told and take whatever salary the city offered, people had to be reminded. That had to be the starting point. Before I went to bed I went into the living room and kissed Mom good night.

"You're really nervous about this demonstration, aren't you?" she said.

"Yeah, I am," I answered.

Thursday morning. Kambui was sitting on my stoop when I got downstairs. I had the signs in a Macy's box. He looked them over and nodded.

I HAVE BEEN DEGRADED

As we walked toward the school, I asked Kambui if he was scared about the demonstration He said no.

"Me, either," I said. "My mom says demonstrations have always worked. At least they'll know we're pissed off."

"I'm not nervous because this one *won't* work," Kambui said. "I'm nervous because they're going to laugh at us, then tomorrow you'll fight Alvin and get beat up, and then we'll get kicked out of school, slide into a life of crime, and go to jail for the rest of our lives. Case closed."

"LaShonda said that a lot of kids were interested," I said. "I just hope that nobody gets mad enough to start a fight."

When Kambui and I got to Da Vinci I could sense that something was already going on. Mr. Culpepper was sitting downstairs at the security desk with the security guard and they were looking around as if they were trying to figure it all out. I knew what had happened. When LaShonda had made her calls somebody had called somebody who had called somebody who had run it all down to Mr. Culpepper.

I took the signs into my homeroom and took some of them out of the box. LaShonda and Bobbi came in and they both took a stack of signs to hand out to the kids who wanted to get involved.

I was hoping for the best as I slipped a string over my head, positioned the sign across my chest, and headed for Algebra.

Math was usually a little interesting, but today was even more interesting because our teacher acted like he didn't care about the signs the black kids were wearing. He just kept talking about how the ancient Egyptians figured out the height of the pyramids.

But the whole time he kept checking out the black kids in the class wearing the signs that said that they were being degraded.

Then, when the class was almost over, Kelly Bena opened the door and blew into the room. She looked around for a hot minute, spotted me, and came to my desk.

"Can I see you outside?" she asked.

I looked over at the teacher and he nodded that I could go. Picking up my books and the signs I had brought with me, I followed her into the hallway.

Kelly stood very close to me and spoke quietly like she always did.

"Zander, I'm not a racist and I don't like being treated like one," she said. Her whole body and face looked mad but she still spoke softly. "This is not fair and I'm going to complain to Mrs. Maxwell!"

"Who said you were a racist?" I asked her.

"Nobody *said* it," Kelly answered. "But if the black kids walking around with signs about being degraded can look at me in the same way that they look at the Sons of the Whatever, then they're putting me in the same category as them, and I resent it."

There were tears running down her face and I knew she wasn't into any acting. I didn't know what to do.

"I'm not saying that you were degrading us."

"Zander, I can see your point. But when you make things this simple — just black against white — you're including everybody," Kelly went on. "And I don't want to be degraded by anyone for who I am or what I am. I go out of my way not to degrade anybody else. If anybody is being degraded, then we're all being degraded."

I handed her a sign.

Kelly looked at the sign and then at me. Her mouth moved as if she was trying to say something, but nothing came out. Then, in one quick movement, she turned the sign around and put it across her chest.

As she walked off I knew it was good and bad. She was saying that the black kids had to own what we were doing the same way that I was saying that Alvin and his crew had to own what they were doing. Okay, but she was also pinning the tail on Alvin, just as I hoped she would.

The period ended and when we went into the hallway there were groups of kids gathered around the bulletin boards where we had put up the broadsheets. It was Mr. Weinstein, the gym teacher, Cody's father, who tore the first one down.

"You've got to put that back up!" I heard Cody say. "It's a school rule that you can't take something down from the bulletin board unless it's obscene."

"Cody, don't you go starting trouble!" Mr. Weinstein said. "Because that's against *my* rules!"

"Put it back up, please!" Cody insisted. "Sir."

Mr. Weinstein dropped the paper on the floor and stormed down the hallway. Cody picked it up and tacked it back onto the bulletin board.

Sidney Aronofsky came up to me and asked me for a sign. Soon I was passing them out to more kids, blacks and whites, girls and boys.

LaShonda had been right. A lot of the kids at Da Vinci had been checking out the Sons of the Confederacy and hadn't liked what they were doing. But they had been quiet until we had given them a way to express themselves. We gave out all of the signs, and before I knew it a lot of students were speaking to me. They were telling me how they were glad that someone was speaking up. One boy said that his grandfather had gone South on a bus with the Freedom Riders.

"He got beaten up," the kid said. "But on the way home he was thinking that was the only fight he had ever won."

In Language Arts, Miss LoBretto changed the lesson to a poem that Yeats had written called "The Second Coming."

"Who knows what Yeats meant when he wrote the lines 'The best lack all conviction, while the worst / Are full of passionate intensity,'" she asked.

We spent the rest of the period talking about Yeats and the poem and about people speaking up when they see something wrong.

I was feeling good when Phat Tony came up to me after Language Arts.

"You're the Zander man," Phat Tony said. "I might even let you join my posse."

"Mr. Scott!"

I turned to see Mr. Culpepper less than four feet away from me. Ashley saw him and came over quickly.

"This is a private conversation, Ashley," Mr. Culpepper was talking through clenched teeth.

"Better make it fast because I just called the city newspapers," Ashley said. "You know, I call them if I have news and they call me if anything big breaks in the city. That's the way we . . ."

I didn't get to hear the rest of what Ashley had to say

because M'r. Culpepper was dragging me down the hall. All the time he was muttering in my ear that I had better stop whatever it was that I was doing or he would personally execute me.

By the time he let me go, we were down near the watercooler outside the recording lab. Mr. Culpepper had me against the wall, his nose a quarter of an inch away from mine, and telling me how much I was going to enjoy the great beyond.

I think he really wanted to do something dramatic, like give me the evil eye and turn me into a frog or something, but in the end he just breathed some really hot breath in my face and walked away.

"Hey, Zander!"

I turned to see Alvin McCraney coming toward me.

"What?"

"I didn't think this was about race, really," he said. He looked uncomfortable. "We were just acting, brother."

"We're just acting, too," I said.

"But guys are saying they don't want to be like me and I didn't mean it to be that way — you know, racist — in the first place," Alvin said.

"That's not the way it seemed to the black kids," I said.

"And I guess most of the white kids saw it that way, too," Alvin said. "Yo, man, I'm, like, sorry and everything."

"Whatever," I said, mostly because I couldn't think of anything else to say.

By the middle of the lunch period Mr. Culpepper had called an assembly of all the eighth-grade students. I asked Ashley when she thought the newspaper reporters would arrive.

"They weren't interested," she said, behind her hand. "There was a fire in the State Office Building and the local reporters are covering that. But, as my grandfather used to say, sometimes even the threat of truth is useful."

From the Poetry Corner of *The Palette*

What Does My Heart See?

By LaShonda Powell

What does my heart see

When I close my eyes to the pain

My sisters must feel?

Does it have secret visions?

Remembered dreamscapes

That twist reality?

What does my heart hear?

When I close my ears to the words

That thunder the air?

Is there some elusive tune

Pulsing through its valves

Like a gone mad iPod

Humming Swahili?

What does my heart feel

When I close my soul to the grief

That stinks up the air?

What sad list of excuses

Can I give myself

Pretending I don't know

How a stone heart breaks?

CHAPTER ELEVEN
Suddenly, Everybody Is a Hero

Mr. Culpepper showed a new talent as he stood on the stage in the auditorium talking to the eighth grade: the ability to turn very red from the top of his upper lip to his forehead while turning just a little red around his chin.

"The entire project is canceled! You will go back to the usual way of dealing with the units on the Civil War. There will be no more Union and Confederate factions. There will be no discussions on slavery outside of the classrooms. There will be no broadsides posted on any bulletin board, student or otherwise, without my permission.

"Anyone who disobeys my directive will face disciplinary action, detention, and possible dismissal from Da Vinci Academy.

"All racial matters will be resolved by me in the privacy of my office! Is there anyone in this assembly who is not clear as to my instructions?"

No one raised their hands.

"To clear the air we can now have any *necessary* comments or observations. Keep your comments brief and to the point!"

Kelly Bena started toward the stage and Mr. Culpepper said she could make her remarks from her seat. She still came to the stage, stood at the mic, and turned toward the kids.

"I don't like to be accused of anything ugly or be associated with anything like being disrespectful to people. Maybe I should have spoken out when I saw what the Sons of the Confederacy published in *The Palette*, but I was trying to be cool because it could have been a freedom of speech issue. It's also a human issue and we can't separate it from our history.

"Also, I don't like the idea that the Cruisers didn't just go after the ones who published the article even though I understand from Zander that it was difficult to pin them down. That's all I have to say except I hope everyone has a nice day."

Alvin came up next.

"I think everybody is still making too much of this whole thing. I'm not saying the Sons of the Confederacy shouldn't have thought more about how people were going to take things, but I know that none of them are racists or anything. We were supposed to be back before the Civil War and we were putting our minds in that time frame.

"I don't know if you have to study history from one point of view. Maybe you can understand it better if you put yourself in someone else's shoes and try to understand what was going on back then.

"I'm sorry for the people I offended but I think it's wrong of people to come down on me so hard when almost the whole country had some connection with slavery back in the day. I guess I'm not too sensitive a guy, but that doesn't mean I'm a bad person. We should be able to talk about race and maybe even make fun of it. Or that might be in a perfect world or something, I don't know. It's, like, a hundred and forty-some years since the Civil War was over and I thought we could treat everything lighter. My bad, but I'm not a racist and I think that Zander should come up and deal with everything people are saying."

A lot of students turned toward me and it was one of those moments when I knew I should have put something down on paper. I hadn't, but I was standing up and headed for the front.

I was thinking hard and fast. The only thing really cool I came up with was that the Cruisers were supposed to have been peacemakers.

Alvin was still at the mic and he held out his hand. I shook it and I heard some boos, probably from the Genius Gangstas.

"Okay, so I would like to thank Mrs. Maxwell for giving us a chance to play a role in studying the Civil War," I said. "I'd like to thank Mr. Culpepper, too. I knew it was hard on him not to come down on us, but he gave us some slack and that was cool. I would like to apologize to anybody that me and the Cruisers got uptight, because we have to own what we did, too. But I don't think you can just throw spit, wipe off your chin, and say you were just kidding.

"If you say something to somebody's face or behind their back or on the Net or on the phone, you have to own it. And that means you have to think about it before it comes out. As for the Sons of the Confederacy, I have to say that you don't have to think wrong to be wrong. Not thinking can be as hard as thinking wrong if it hurts people.

"I'd like to thank the Cruisers for their support and how generally cool they are. I'd also like to thank the Genius Gangstas and all the kids who supported us.

"Da Vinci is the Da Bomb!"

I got some nice props, and when Mrs. Maxwell clapped even Mr. Culpepper put his hands together — once. Mrs. Maxwell came up to the mic next.

"Well, haven't we had an adventure?" she said. "I think we've all learned something very valuable. Because speech is free in America it is still very powerful and must be handled with caution. I think we've also learned that there are many issues surrounding the major events of history that make problem solving difficult.

"I'm very proud of the fact that, although some tempers were pushed to a high degree, the issues were resolved in thoughtful ways. The debates were very similar to what occurred during the period before the Civil War.

"I would like to thank those students who represented the Union, those who represented the Confederacy, and even those who represented other groups. The Cruisers' peacemaking efforts did bring the arguments forward, but sometimes, as Mr. Culpepper suggested, there comes a time when we need to change the path of history. I hope part of your classroom instructions on the War between the States will also include some discussions about what happened with our little exercise. Lastly, I want you all to be very proud of yourselves. While there were disagreements, there was also a great deal of learning going on and it was handled with typical Da Vinci dignity. Thank you. Now, please return to your next scheduled period."

When we left the auditorium a lot of kids came up and gave me high fives. They hadn't spoken up before but now they were in on it and I guess that's the way things go. People who should be taking a stand won't budge until they're pushed into it. It was seriously lame but I didn't say anything. I wondered what I would have done if it had been about somebody besides black people.

If I had been white would I have spoken up? Was it really just about the principles or was it mostly about the personal hurt?

Everybody was buzzing as if a thousand lightbulbs had gone off in their heads, and I was thinking it was easy being a hero when you weren't really risking anything in the first place.

In US History Mr. Siegfried gave the speech we all expected.

"Most studies of the years leading up to the Civil War are notable for the fact that they move the human issues away from the center of the discussions. The statements of the Southern states declaring their reasons for leaving the Union talk about constitutional rights to own slaves and constitutional obligations of the Northern states to return escaped slaves, but they carefully avoid talking about the simple moral issues. Is it right to enslave a human being?

"What happened was that a number of fantasies were created. The first was that Africans were better off as slaves in America than they would have been as free people in Africa. The second fantasy was that most people in the South believed in a Southern cause that included slavery. Most people in the South never owned a slave and didn't want the war. The war made them victims of the slave trade.

"This is not 1860, and we can't turn back the clock to a different time and different mentality. In the final analysis I think the Cruisers did a good job in centering the issues.

In theory they stopped the Civil War. Now for your home-work assignment."

The groans flew around the room.

"I want you to write essays about what would have hap-pened if there actually had been no Civil War," Mr. Siegfried went on.

The Cruisers got a short round of applause at the end of the class and I felt good about the whole thing because we had stopped the bad feelings flying around the school, and we did get kids to work with us in the end, so it was mostly good. In the media center there were some other ideas.

"I think we should have let Zander and Alvin fight it out," Cody was saying. "Then we could see what the Zander man has going on."

"I think Zander would have won easy," LaShonda said. "He's got those long arms and everything."

"I still don't know if this whole thing is settled," Kambui said. "Because some people were talking in the auditorium and being all correct, but they were hanging out after-ward and I think they were backing off and going back to thinking they were right, it was all light stuff."

We talked more about everything later when we were walking home.

"Time will tell," I said.

"*Time will tell?*" Kambui stopped in the middle of the street and turned to me. "You got that from *The Book of Lame Sayings?*"

Bobbi and LaShonda came over and we all exchanged high fives.

"We are so together!" LaShonda said.

"I think that even Mr. Culpepper has to admit it," Bobbi said.

I doubted that.

When I got home Mom was crying again.

"I just got off the phone with your father," she said.

"And?"

"He's having the subpoena dropped," she said. "He said he was very upset about his conversation with you and thought that I was poisoning your mind against him and his new wife. He doesn't want you going to Seattle."

"So I'm staying in Harlem."

"Yeah."

"So what you crying about?"

"I always feel so bad when I talk with him," she said. "You know that."

"Did you tell him you were going to be in a movie?"

"I did, and I told him I was going to be making twice as much money as I am," Mom said.

"Why did you say that?"

"To make him feel bad," she said. "You think I should call him up and apologize for lying?"

We both said "naaah!" at the same time.

THE PALETTE

A TIME TO LOVE . . .

By Ashley Schmidt

In thinking over the events of the last few weeks I was so very proud to see that Zander Scott and his merry band of Cruisers were able to bring about a settled peace between the proposed belligerents in the Civil War. I thought to myself how wonderful it would have been if Zander had been around in the 1850s. How many thousands of lives would have been saved, and how much heartache would have been prevented?

But then in the middle of my personal celebration as a lover of peace I began to think that perhaps for hundreds of thousands of enslaved Africans the war served a useful purpose. Through the Emancipation Proclamation and the subsequent Union victory, the grounds for the ending of slavery were established. As much as I hate war I believe it is preferable to being enslaved.

Curled up in my bed while outlining an editorial praising the Cruisers, I came to the conclusion that Zander might have actually been wrong if they had really stopped the Civil War. The next question that came to mind was, how many other events that we now accept as either good or bad could be seen differently from another point of view? Perhaps there is a time to make love and a time to make war after all.

Was the western expansion in the nineteenth century good for all Americans? Was the fall of the Roman Empire a universal disaster? How about the defeat of the Spanish Armada? Was the fall of the tsar of Russia really so wonderful? How about the war on drugs? Will the end of death, if we can ever achieve it, be the completely positive idea it seems to be? *The Palette* invites its readers to submit examples of historical events that might be viewed differently from a slightly altered perspective. The three most original (with suitable citations!) will be published in *The Palette*.

Meanwhile, I still have to offer my congrats to Zander and the Cruisers.

COMING UP NEXT . . . THE SECOND BOOK IN THE CRUISERS SERIES

KING'S GAMBIT

It's one thing to rock the power of your pen; it's another to crack a code. In the second book of the Cruisers series, the term "Gifted and Talented" takes on a whole new meaning for Zander and his friends.

Here's the beginning of how they roll in King's Gambit.

PICTURE PERFECT

"**Y**o, Kambui, I was thinking about Sidney," I said. "I just can't imagine him with a drug problem."

"What are you doing?"

"Trying to figure out Sidney Aronofsky's problem," I said.

"No, I mean right now. You sitting at the table? You eating a sandwich? What are you doing?"

"I'm lying on the floor right next to my dumbbells thinking maybe I'll get to some exercises," I said. "What you doing?"

"I'm texting Zhade Hopkins," Kambui said. "I'm thinking about asking her to go out with me."

"Zhade is too fine for you," I said.

"No, I think she digs me," Kambui said. "I think you and I should go out with her and her sister. On a double date."

"Where do you want to take them?"

"Never mind, she just texted me back and called me a frog," Kambui said. "Why did she have to go there?"

"Maybe she's hoping to kiss you and turn you into a handsome prince," I said.

"I didn't like her anyway."

Lie.

"So, getting back to Sidney," I went on. "I think he knows drugs are bad but he hasn't really seen how bad so he's, like, into some kind of movie version."

"What movie?"

"I don't know, man, *some* movie," I said. "It's like you see guys get shot in pictures and then the next day you see them on television talking about how good the film was. It makes the killing part not too bad."

"So you think we should get him some heavy drugs and let him OD or something?" Kambui asked.

"This afternoon I told him that we wanted to publish a picture of a crackhead in *The Cruiser*," I said. "I asked him if he could get us one."

"Look, Zander, I know you and Sidney are friends," Kambui said. "But as far as I'm concerned he's just weirding out. Maybe all that chess he plays has got his head twisted. You know — mad genius stuff."

"The guy's a chess wizard," I said. "Plus he's a good guy and he goes to our school. I was shocked when he got arrested for buying marijuana. If he does come up with a picture I'm going to put it in *The Cruiser*."

"I don't see how it's going to help," Kambui said. "But it doesn't cost anything, so why not?"

"I have to do *something*," I said.

"I got to get to my homework," Kambui said. "I have fifteen thousand more pages to read."

"You think if I texted Zhade and asked her about us double-dating with her and her sister she might say yes?" I asked.

"I wouldn't even go out with her now," Kambui said. "Where did she get that frog bit?"

"That was kind of cold," I said.

Kambui said he had to finish his homework and would see me in school. When I had hung up it was easy to see that Kambui was more into Zhade then he was into Sidney's problems. But Kambui was my main man and I knew he would be thinking about it. That's the way he is. You say something to him and you think he's forgotten about it and then two or three weeks later — *bam!* — he's right back on the case.

I was still lying on the floor when Mom came to the door and pointed to the cell phone she was holding. Somebody was calling for me and she wanted to know if I wanted to answer it. She put the phone behind her back and said it was a lady.

For a wild moment I thought it was going to be Zhade. Zhade is so hot she can melt a Hershey bar from across the room by just looking at it. It wasn't Zhade, it was Bobbi.

"Hey, Zander, I've got the game with Powell all figured out." She was chirping again. She does that when she's happy. "I have four numbers. If we manage to get three of them we'll win."

"The first number is one," I said. "If we get one more point than the other team we'll win."

"The first number is nine," Bobbi continued, ignoring me. "One player has to get nine rebounds. The second number —"

"Why nine?" I asked.

"The second number is seventy. That has to be our free throw percentage."

"Where are you getting these numbers?"

"Each number represents a phase of the game that we have to dominate," she said.

"You're not playing, Bobbi," I said. "We're playing."

"I'm giving you the tools to win the game," Bobbi said. "So it's nine rebounds by one player, seventy percent of our free throws, the third is team assists — we need nine — and the last number is thirty-five. We need to hit thirty-five percent of our three-point tries. That's it. What do you think?"

"Bobbi, you don't know diddly-squat about basketball," I said.

"Yeah, I do," Bobbi said. "Because it's really about numbers and percentages."

"So what do you think about Sidney's problem?"

"What do you think about my math solution?"

"We'll check it out when we play Powell Thursday," I said. "And if we get those numbers and lose we'll burn you at the stake."

"And if you win you can put a photo of me in the trophy case," Bobbi said.

"Can we get back to Sidney and chess?" I asked.

"He's the best chess player on our team," Bobbi said. "I'm second board, John Brendel is third, and Todd Balf is fourth."

"I could probably beat all of you with my eyes closed," I said.

"In your dreams, baby," Bobbi said. "In your dreams!"

Okay, the basketball team, Bobbi, LaShonda, Kambui, and Ashley Schmidt from the school newspaper, *The Palette*, went to 128th Street and Amsterdam Avenue to play against Adam Clayton Powell. On the way, Bobbi kept passing around her numbers.

"Zander, you have to get the nine rebounds," she said. "You're the tallest."

"The secret to basketball," Coach Law said, "is having the will to win. Without that will you're going to lose."

"Numbers don't lie," Bobbi said. "Numbers are a way of God slipping the truth to us on the QT."

"Spoken like a true young lady," Coach Law said.

"Spoken like a sexist basketball coach," LaShonda said.

Coach Law grinned.

Adam Clayton Powell Academy's basketball team was okay but I didn't like them because the whole school thought they were hot stuff. They had had Mae Jamison come up to the school once, and President Clinton and some author from New Jersey, so they thought they were special.

"Can you get nine boards?" Cody asked me.

"Yeah."

"If you keep crashing the boards you'll get fouled," Cody said. "I'll drive more down the lane so I should pick up a couple of fouls, and the whole team will work on assists."

Coach Law kept talking about the will to win and Cody kept looking at Bobbi's numbers. I was wondering if Cody was going soft on Bobbi. Ashley had a copy of Bobbi's numbers, too, and she wanted to write them up in *The Palette*.

The game started and I gave up everything to work on the boards. The dude I was up against, a West Indian brother I knew, was strong and did a lot of pushing but he couldn't really sky. I was snatching bounds pretty easy.

The whole thing was that all of us went into the game

with Bobbi's numbers in our heads. It was a little freaky at first, but I didn't want to fall down on my count.

In the end we beat them. No, we crushed them. Okay, we left them bleeding and whimpering on the court! Cody scored thirty points and was getting so mean I had to help Powell defend him. I only scored sixteen points because I'm a merciful kind of guy.

I felt great about the game and especially about beating Powell. But the way that Ashley wrote it up in *The Palette* you would have thought that Bobbi beat Powell all by herself.

I saw Kambui in the media center and he asked me if Bobbi was going to replace me on the team.

"I just hope the coach doesn't fall in love with those numbers," I said.

"Did Sidney show up with a picture of a crackhead?"

"No, he gave me a picture of a chess board with numbers on it," I said. "Very strange."

y cousin says that sometimes people keep hanging on to a symbol that comforts them," LaShonda said. "So maybe Sidney showed up with that picture of a chess board because he's only comfortable around chess."

"No," Bobbi answered. "It's not just a picture, it's a coded message."

Can you crack it?